WEEKLY READER CHILDREN'S BOOK CLUB PRESENTS

The Muppets Take Manhattan

A MOVIE STORYBOOK

**Starring
Jim Henson's Muppets™**

Muppet Press/Random House

JIM HENSON PRESENTS
A Frank Oz Film

The Muppets Take Manhattan

Starring the Muppet Performers

Jim Henson
Frank Oz
Dave Goelz
Steve Whitmire
Richard Hunt
Jerry Nelson

Still Photographer Kerry Hayes

Executive Producer Jim Henson

Screenplay by Frank Oz and
Tom Patchett and Jay Tarses

Story by Tom Patchett and Jay Tarses

Produced by David Lazer

Directed by Frank Oz

Storybook Adaptation by Danny Abelson

Copyright © 1984 by Henson Associates, Inc.
THE MUPPETS TAKE MANHATTAN, THE MUPPET SHOW, MUPPET,
and MUPPET character names are trademarks of Henson Associates, Inc.
All rights reserved under International and Pan-American Copyright Conventions.
Published in the United States by Random House, Inc., New York, and simultaneously
in Canada by Random House of Canada Limited, Toronto.
A Muppet Press Book produced by Henson Organization
Publishing in association with Random House, Inc.

Library of Congress Cataloging in Publication Data:
Abelson, Danny, 1950– The Muppets take Manhattan. SUMMARY: When the Muppets
graduate from college, they take to the streets of New York, searching
for a way to get their senior variety show on Broadway.
[1. Plays—Fiction. 2. New York (N.Y.)—Fiction. 3. Puppets—Fiction] I. Muppets take Manhattan.
II. Title. PZ7.A1597Mu 1984 [E] 83-19153 ISBN: 0-394-86386-0 (trade); 0-394-96386-5 (lib. bdg.)
Manufactured in the United States of America 1 2 3 4 5 6 7 8 9 0

This book is a presentation of
Weekly Reader Children's Book Club.
Weekly Reader Children's Book Club offers book clubs for children from preschool through junior high school.

For further information write to:
Weekly Reader Children's Book Club
4343 Equity Drive
Columbus, Ohio 43228

Weekly Reader Books offers several exciting card and activity programs. For information,
write to WEEKLY READER BOOKS, P.O. Box 16636,
Columbus, Ohio 43216.

The Muppets Take Manhattan

It was the last day of the term and the Muppets were graduating from college. Up on the stage of the college auditorium Kermit the Frog and his fellow performers were coming to the end of "Manhattan Melodies," the senior class variety show. As a packed house watched, Miss Piggy danced daintily across the stage, Scooter and Fozzie harmonized, and Rowlf the dog howled away happily. Gonzo was . . . well, he was gonzoing for all he was worth with his adored chicken, Camilla, by his side.

Then Dr. Teeth and the Electric Mayhem Band played the last crashing chords and the curtain came down on the show's big finale.

And the audience went wild! They clapped, they whistled, they stamped and cheered, and then they clapped some more. Cries of "Author! Author!" rang out, first once or twice and then over and over again. In the wings the author hung back modestly, but the other performers convinced him to take a bow by shoving and pulling him out onto the stage.

And there he stood, blushing a kind of reddish green, the president of the senior class and author of "Manhattan Melodies"—Kermit the Frog. "Way to go, Kermit!" and "What a frog!" his classmates called out to him over the thunderous applause. Kermit was overcome. It felt wonderful to have an audience clapping for the show he was so proud of. "See you on Broadway," yelled someone from the audience. Kermit laughed at the thought. Then he bowed one last time and ducked back into the wings.

"Why not?" Scooter asked the others backstage. "Why don't we put the show on Broadway?"

Miss Piggy, who was still swooning with happiness at seeing her adored Kermy taking his bows, suddenly woke up. "Broadway!" she exclaimed, her eyes lighting up like giant searchlights. "*Moi* can see it already!"

"Yeah!" agreed Fozzie. "Broadway must be dying to get a show like this."

"Broadway! Broadway!" chanted Animal, the wild-eyed drummer of the Electric Mayhem Band.

"But the show isn't good enough for Broadway," said Kermit.

"Not good enough!" chorused the others. "It's more than good enough. It's great!"

"It's a tempting idea," said Kermit. "But we have to think about our plans for the future."

And then Fozzie had a brilliant idea. "So I guess if we don't go to Broadway, we just have to . . ." He paused, looking as sad and forlorn as a bear can look. ". . . we just have to say good-bye to one another." He waited for the words to sink in.

Kermit looked around at each of his friends. The thought of the gang breaking up and heading off in different directions was painful. No one spoke, and Fozzie held his breath. "Well!" Kermit said at last. "What are we waiting for? We're going to Broadway!"

Before anyone had time to say "Are you *sure*?" or "Maybe we shouldn't rush in to this" or "Help!!" the gang was there, gazing in awe at the famous Manhattan skyline. Right in front of their very noses was the Empire State Building, as pretty as a picture. And there was an excellent reason why it was as pretty as a picture—it *was* a picture! It hung on the wall of the not very clean bus terminal that was the only part of Manhattan they had seen so far.

The terminal wasn't much, but it

was home. They decided to stay in their lockers that night, even if the lockers weren't exactly first-class accommodations. "More like *twenty-first* class," said Fozzie. "Right up there with park benches."

"But it's just for one night," said Piggy. "Because we'll all be big Broadway stars tomorrow."

"No problem," said Gonzo, whose personal habits have often been described as "unusual" and even more often as "really, *really* weird." "This is much better than the file cabinet I used to live in."

"Squawk," agreed Camilla, and everyone else settled down to sleep.

It was early the next morning that an excited group of college graduates set out to find fame and fortune. Their first stop was the office of Mr. Martin Price, producer. "His office is so close to Broadway, he *must* be an important producer," Scooter remarked as they made their way in.

"We saw Mr. Price's name in the paper and we have a show called 'Manhattan Melodies,'" Kermit explained to the secretary.

"A frog with a musical to see you," she called out over the intercom. The gang couldn't believe their luck when an immediate "Show them in" came right back from Mr. Price.

Mr. Price had an extremely large and important-looking office with an extremely large and important-looking desk. Kermit didn't want to waste any of this extremely important man's time.

"Hit it!" he signaled the others, and as Janice and Floyd played their instruments and the others sang and hummed behind him, he launched into one of the bounciest numbers from the show.

"Frog! Frog!" Mr. Price shouted. "No singing, okay?" They all froze, and Kermit had to think fast. He didn't want to ruin this golden opportunity, so he quickly began to tell the producer about the story of the show.

"It's about life in the big city," he started.

"Terrific! You mean cops and

shooting and stuff?" the producer asked.

"Uh, no . . . songs and dances, actually," Kermit corrected him.

"Okay . . . and there are lots of big names in it, right?"

"Actually," Kermit said, feeling sure that this would be the end of the interview, "actually, we're going to be the stars."

"You know what?" Mr. Price asked, sniffing the air. "I smell something! I smell . . . a hit! Fellas, I'd be proud to produce you on Broadway."

They could hardly believe their ears. "We did it!" Kermit said as the words sank in. "Great!" Scooter exclaimed. "It's too good to be true!" exclaimed Gonzo. "I can hardly believe it," added Fozzie.

"Now all you have to do is give me three hundred dollars each," said the producer, "and we'll get started."

"Did someone say 'too good to be true'?" asked Kermit sadly, realizing that they had been tricked.

"Kermy," Piggy whispered. "I don't think that's quite right. Isn't *he* supposed to pay *us*?"

Suddenly the door to the office burst open and two policemen and an elderly lady came charging in. "That's him!" the lady shouted angrily, pointing to the producer. "That's Murray Plotsky. I gave him my life savings."

"All right, Murray, you've pulled your last con job," said one of the cops. "This time you're going away for good."

"Murray?" Fozzie whispered to Kermit. "I thought his name was Martin."

Suddenly Plotsky made a diving leap for Camilla. "One more step and the chicken gets it," he sneered to the policemen.

"No!" cried Gonzo. "Take me instead." The crook grabbed Gonzo by the nose and backed out of the door with both of them—Gonzo *and* his beloved chicken.

It was then that Floyd had a brilliant idea. "Animal," he whispered to the ferocious drummer. "Bad man." And he pointed after Murray. A wild look came into Animal's eyes. With a ferocious roar, he tore off after the crook.

A few seconds, a hideous crash, and three or four awful screams later, the quaking Plotsky hobbled back into the room. "Arrest me, please," he begged the policemen. "These animals are crazy!" Animal grinned proudly, a piece of Plotsky's trousers dangling from his teeth.

Gonzo comforted the shaken Camilla, and Kermit rallied the others. "We're going to get this show on Broadway," he told the others cheerfully, and led the way out of the office.

But it wasn't going to be all that easy. In the next few weeks Kermit and his friends found out that producers are geniuses when it comes to saying no. They met one producer who could say no while shaving, and two others who didn't even have to look up from their newspapers to know they weren't interested in "Manhattan Melodies." Another producer didn't even have to say a word—he just turned out the lights and left the

room while the Muppets were singing for him. One simply fell asleep,
and the cleverest of them all managed
to eat lunch, talk on the telephone,
and doze off while the gang was singing. And he still managed to say no
by gesturing toward the door with his
chin between snores!

Soon the weeks became months.
They were still living in the bus terminal and still getting nowhere. The
streets of New York, which once had
seemed so exciting and busy, now
seemed noisy and unfriendly. Their
hopes, their money, *everything*
seemed to be running out, and all the
responses from all the producers
seemed to add up to one gigantic
"No!"—a "no" bigger than the Empire State Building and louder than a
thousand doors slamming in their
faces.

It was a sad and bad-tempered group of Muppets who slouched along the sidewalk one hot summer night. Kermit felt worst of all because he felt responsible for all the others.

"Maybe we could sell the script if you wrote in some great special effects, like exploding socks," suggested Gonzo.

"Lame idea," commented Janice.

"Oh, yeah?" Gonzo snapped back.

"Don't yell at her!" yelled Floyd.

"Stop making trouble," added Scooter, and anyone who felt like it joined in the argument.

"Kermit, tell them to stop bickering," Piggy pleaded.

"What do you think?" Scooter asked, tugging at Kermit's arm.

"Yeah, Kermit," the others chimed in. "What do you think we should do?"

And suddenly it was all too much. Too much pressure, too much responsibility, too much of his friends arguing because they were tired and losing hope. Kermit—quiet, gentle President of the Class Kermit—exploded. *"I don't know!!"* he shouted. "I don't know what to do next! We failed . . . we tried and we failed!" And he sagged, too miserable to yell anymore.

"We may as well eat," he suggested in a quiet, sad voice, and the others followed him in to Pete's, the luncheonette they happened to be passing. When they were seated, a waiter came to take their orders. This waiter was a little different from most other waiters. He was a rat named Rizzo.

"Kermit! The waiter is a rat," hissed Fozzie as Rizzo approached.

"What'll you have?" Rizzo asked.

"The number for the Board of Health," Floyd snickered.

The waiter threw down his tiny tray in disgust. "That does it! Another rat joke! I work my whiskers off twenty, sometimes twenty-nine hours a day for tips, and you act like I got no feelings!" The rat began to sob, and Fozzie immediately put his arm around the poor fellow.

"Gee . . . we're really sorry. We know how it is. We don't have any money either."

The waiter suddenly stopped sniffing. "Sorry. Not my table," he snapped, and walked away.

"What a rat," remarked Fozzie,

trying very hard to drown out the sounds of a bear stomach growling in hunger.

Just then Kermit looked up to see a pretty young woman come running through the door. "Sorry I'm late, Pop," she called breathlessly to Pete, the owner. "But you'll be so proud of me. I passed the test!" She pulled on a uniform as Pete put a hamburger and a glass of milk down on the hatch.

"Jenny, very rapid quick hurrying with cow juice and patty taking to lady," he said.

Kermit heard this and got the distinct impression that Pete was not a native New Yorker. He got up and walked over to the hatch. "We'll take eleven bowls of the soup, please," Kermit said to Pete. "But there is one thing I should tell you. We've got this show that's going to be a big hit on Broadway. But right now we're all broke."

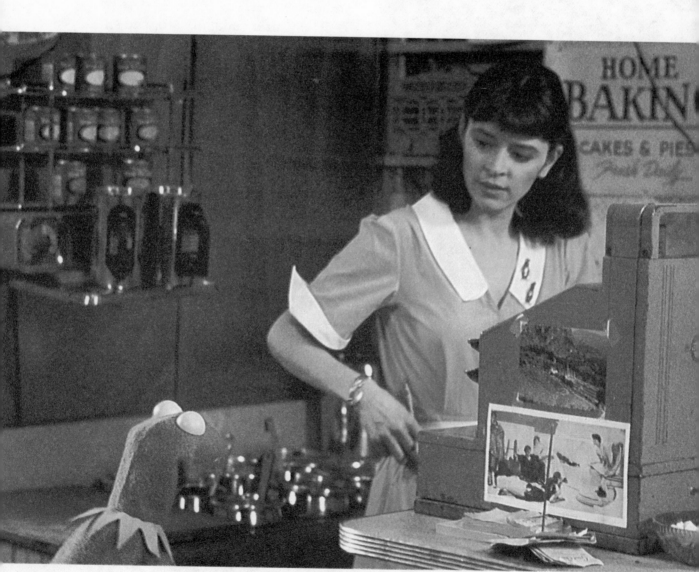

Pete stopped, gave Kermit a strange look, and leaned very close to him. "I tell you what is. Big city is no buildings, no subway choo-choo, no Cadillac bus. Big city is peoples . . . is dancing . . . is tomatoes, is music . . . yes? Peoples is peoples, okay?"

Pete went back into the kitchen, and Kermit shrugged and started walking back to the table. He was getting pretty used to rejection. Then Jenny took his arm. "Wait . . . I just know my father is back there getting soup for you and your friends right now." There was something about her

smile that made Kermit, worried and hungry though he was, smile back. Kermit had the feeling that they would be spending quite a bit of time at Pete's Luncheonette.

While he and Jenny were chatting, a very different kind of discussion was going on at the table. Piggy was the only one not joining in, because she was too busy watching her frog.

"I feel terrible about Kermit," Fozzie told the others.

"Me, too," agreed Scooter. "We put too much pressure on him."

Floyd nodded sadly. "The frog was

19

right, back there . . . we do depend on him too much.''

"Maybe if we all went out on our own, it would make things easier for him,'' Scooter suggested, and no one disagreed.

Piggy didn't say anything. She was straining to hear Kermit and Jenny. She heard Jenny say that she planned to go to fashion design school. *I'd like you to leave for design school right now!* Piggy thought. *A school nice and far from Kermit . . . in Siberia, for instance, or even better, on the moon!*

"If we all go away and get jobs,'' Scooter was saying at that moment, "Kermit will be really proud of us.''

This time Piggy heard. "But I can't leave him!" she wailed. "We're pinned!"

There was no time for anyone to respond, because just then Kermit arrived back at the table.

"Well, Kermit," Scooter announced. "We've had some job offers."

"Right!" the others chimed in. "Terrific offers."

"Great!" said Kermit. "So we'll have the money to repaint our lockers at the terminal."

Scooter had to think fast. "The offers are all out of town," he stammered.

"That's right . . . way out of town," added Fozzie, backing him up, and the others all nodded their agreement.

"Piggy, are you going too?" Kermit asked softly.

She whimpered pathetically. "Yes," she finally managed to say.

"We'll all write to you," said Fozzie.

"And we all believe in the show," added Scooter, realizing that he was only making everyone feel worse.

The good friends looked sadly at one another. No one knew what else to say. "Well . . . gee," Kermit stammered as Piggy fought back her tears. "So that's it, I guess."

"Guess so," agreed Scooter.

"Yep," added Fozzie, who suddenly couldn't look Kermit in the eye.

Kermit shrugged, trying to look cheerful. "Well, then," he announced, "I guess that's that."

The very next day the group split up to go their separate ways. Fozzie had his teddy bear with him as he hopped a freight train heading north, and Gonzo and the chicken of his

dreams, Camilla, bounced around on the back of a truck going due west. Scooter set off alone on his bike. Rowlf rode the bus out of town, and Dr. Teeth and the Electric Mayhem Band hitched a ride on the highway.

At the train station Kermit ran along the platform as Piggy waved from the window of her compartment. The train gathered speed, pulled out of the station, and then suddenly Kermit was left alone. Alone in the middle of a railway station in the middle of a big city.

22

It was a forlorn frog who wandered around the streets of New York that night, too lost in his lonely thoughts to notice where he was heading. When he looked up and realized he was at the base of the Empire State Building, Kermit decided to go in and ride to the top.

Up, way up on the observation deck, he looked down on the city. He felt very sad at losing his friends. But he felt something else, too. Determination. In a small but defiant voice he addressed the millions of lights twinkling below him. "I'm going to get my friends back and we're going to make it on Broadway!" Kermit shouted into the night. "Do you hear me? I'm staying and I'm going to make it!"

Far below, at the bottom of the immense skyscraper, a mysterious figure waited in the shadows. A fedora, the favorite hat of mysterious figures, was pulled down low, hiding the mysterious figure's face. Then the mysterious figure stepped out of the shadows and looked upward. Beneath the hat was a familiar face, with familiar long eyelashes and a familiar snout. Piggy had returned to be near her frog!

Early the next morning Kermit went to see Pete to ask him for a job. But Rizzo was there before him, with a whole troop of his rat friends. "I gotta have these guys to help," Rizzo was telling Pete as Kermit walked in.

"Okay, you work," Pete told the rats. "But I tell you what is ... is jumping ... is cheese ... is big show ... yes, no, and maybe for sure ... okay?"

"Okay, Pete!" chorused the rats, and they scampered off to work.

Kermit finally got his chance. "I'll do anything!" he told Pete desperately, but Pete seemed too busy to listen. "I'll sweep up . . . clean windows . . . anything!" Kermit began to get the feeling that it was hopeless. Then Jenny walked in.

"Pop . . . we could use some help in the kitchen," she told her father.

Pete thought for a moment and then turned to Kermit. "Okay is dishes need washing. Is job of plenty wet soapsuds bubbling, yes?"

"Yes, Pete!" replied Kermit, grateful to him and especially to Jenny. "And thanks!"

Later he told Jenny about how his friends had had to leave town. "But I'm going to sell the show so I can bring them all back. I've been reading up on producers and now I know what I have to do."

"I really admire you for doing what you believe in," Jenny told him. "Someday I want to do something special in fashion designing too. Someday."

Kermit looked up from the dishes he was washing. "You know," he said slowly, "I think your fashion designing might be able to help me now. I've got a three-part plan to sell the show. The first part is, if you can't beat 'em, join 'em."

A few days later an extremely bizarre-looking frog bounced into the offices of the William Morris Agency. Thanks to Jenny's help, Kermit had been transformed into the slickest-looking frog in the history of frogs in show business. In a flashy shirt open to the navel, even flashier bell-bottom jeans, bright white loafers, and dazzling gold jewelry around his neck, Kermit was wearing sunglasses to protect himself from the glare of his own outfit!

"Hiya, sweetheart," he called breezily to the receptionist. "I got an appointment with your theater agent here."

"Leonard Winesop?" she asked.

"Yeah . . . Lennie, right," said Kermit, who had never heard the name before. "We go *way* back! I'll just go right in." Before she could stop him, he went bounding down the hallway, bell-bottoms flapping away.

"Lennie! Sweetheart! Babe!" he called to the agent as he burst through the door. "My private plane's double-parked, so I gotta run, but I'm giving

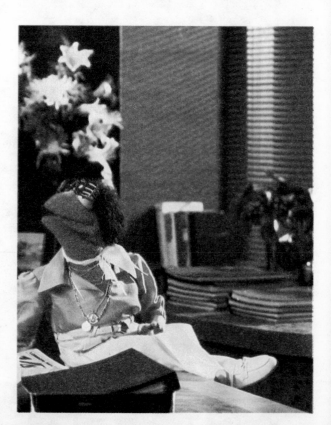

you this boffo, socko script, 'Manhattan Melodies.' " He shoved the script into the agent's hand and slapped him on the back. "I gotta split, babe . . . but remember, boffo! socko!" Kermit called as he bowed out the door.

As he left the building, feeling hopeful and excited, Kermit had no way of knowing that the agent had already tossed the script into the wastebasket.

A few minutes later Kermit met Jenny. As he told her what had happened, he had no way of knowing about something else: They were being watched. Across the road, a figure lurked, trying very hard not to be seen. It was Miss Piggy, wearing dark glasses and a trench coat, the favorite outfit of those who are trying very hard not to be seen. Two muscular construction workers were trying to flirt with her as she strained to hear what Jenny and Kermit were talking about.

As she watched the pair like a hawk,

Miss Piggy saw Jenny give Kermit a hug. She didn't know that it was just a little friendly encouragement; she decided to turn into an exploding pig first and ask questions later. She smashed an empty oil drum, then picked up a lead pipe and bent it like a pretzel! The construction workers, who had been calling "Hey, baby!" and "Over here, cute thing" to this extremely dangerous character, grew very quiet and quickly went back to work.

Piggy was still breathing fire when

she rushed into an elegant store nearby and hurried to the cosmetics counter. Her new boss was not very thrilled that she had returned late from lunch on her very first day of work.

She apologized halfheartedly, and he stalked off in a huff.

"What's wrong, Piggy?" asked her new friend, Eileen, who worked at the cosmetics counter with her.

Piggy told Eileen what had happened. "But I'm going to fight for my frog," she vowed. "You do think I'm pretty enough, don't you?"

"Of course," said Eileen.

"Gorgeous?"

Eileen's face fell.

"All right," said Piggy with a sigh. "How about trustworthy?"

"You're better than gorgeous," Eileen reassured her. "You're unique.

But you *could* use a little rouge."

She sat Piggy down at the cosmetics counter and dabbed a little rouge on her cheeks. And then she added some eyeliner. "Oops! Maybe I went just a little bit too far," Eileen said.

"More!" Piggy commanded fearlessly. Then Eileen *really* went to work with an eyebrow pencil and lipstick and glitter and polka dots and practically anything else that wasn't locked away. When Piggy looked up, her face resembled an explosion in a paint factory. But that wasn't what she noticed first. What first caught her attention was her boss. He was staring at her, and he was furious.

He had surprisingly little to say about the way Piggy looked. Just a few words. Three, to be precise: "You are fired."

Meanwhile, miles away from the big city, the other Muppets were having problems too. In the tiny, polka-crazy town of Monongahela, Pennsylvania, Dr. Teeth and the Electric Mayhem Band were performing at the local Firemen's Bazaar. The band was just getting ready to play another polka.

"All right! Here's another down-home polka for you polka-crazy cats and kittens," Floyd announced from the bandstand. The other band members groaned. It was their eighty-ninth polka of the evening.

"Like . . . I'm not totally sure my vibes will survive," Janice whispered.

"I think I'm polka'd out."

Just then Floyd was approached by two strange-looking characters. Dr. Bunsen Honeydew introduced himself and his assistant, Beaker. "We couldn't help but notice that your drummer has been playing a mite out of tempo," the scientist told Floyd.

"Animal is wiggin' out. Polkas just ain't his thing," Floyd admitted.

"Luckily for you," said Dr. Honeydew, "I have my gas-powered drumometer here, which plugs directly into the drummer's brain." Beaker held up a weird-looking device.

"If you can find his brain, sure," said Floyd, and the strange cap was put on Animal's head. Dr. Honeydew started the motor, Floyd gave the signal, and the band launched into the "How Come They Never Get Tired of the Polka?" polka.

But in a few moments Animal was slowing down, so Dr. Honeydew instructed Beaker to turn the motor up. When he did, Animal started drumming faster and faster, making the dancers spin around at a crazy speed. His eyes lit up like fireworks, smoke poured out of his ears, and he bashed his drums harder and harder, faster and faster. He drummed in double time, he drummed in double triple time, and then suddenly there was a terrific explosion and Animal stared out from under the blackened, smoking cap on his head. "One more time!" he yelled, and then slowly fell over.

Way up north, in the remote, quiet, peaceful woods of Maine, Fozzie Bear would have given anything to have been with his friends, even with an exploding drummer in their midst. Fozzie had decided to hibernate with the other bears. But he was realizing that being the only one awake was very lonely, especially when the nap lasted three months!

I wish I weren't too shy to do something, he thought. *Like yell "All you boring, snoring bears WAKE UP!!"* Just then another bear bumped against him and opened her eyes.

"Hello," she said pleasantly.

"Gee," replied Fozzie shyly, "I didn't know this cave was coed." Before he had time to panic, the friendly she-bear had snuggled against him, closed her eyes, and gone to sleep.

And off in Michigan, Gonzo and his chicken companion-for-life, Camilla, were all set to perform their indescribable Aqua Show.

"I will now describe the indescribable show," Gonzo announced to the audience from his takeoff platform. "After skiing thrilling and intricate patterns through the slalom course, I will make a death-defying leap from the ramp, hurtle through the Circle of Doom loop-the-loop, and land effortlessly upon my easy chair while my chickens sing 'Do You Know the Way to San Jose?' " He turned to the boat driver. "Ready!" he called, and then stopped to give his goggles one last wipe.

That was a big mistake. Because just then the boat roared off, and Gonzo was yanked forward by the rope. Camilla and her fellow chicken choir members sang their hearts out, the crowd yawned, and Gonzo was dragged through the water at a hundred miles per hour, screaming his unusually shaped head off. "Help!! I have an unusual fear of serious injury!" he yelled. "And also a fear of early death!!"

Back in New York, Kermit finished reading the postcards from Gonzo in Michigan and Fozzie in Maine and Dr. Teeth and the gang in Pennsylvania.

"Gee, Kermit, you look worried," Jenny remarked.

"Still no word from Piggy," Kermit said, shaking his head. He sighed a deep, sad sigh. "If I could only sell the show," he said, looking very glum.

"Of course you will!" Jenny reassured him. Then she gave Kermit a hug.

Across the street Piggy was watching through binoculars. Did she realize that Jenny was hugging Kermit just to cheer him up? Did she like what she saw? Judging from the terrible, bloodcurdling scream and the smashing, crashing sound of pure pig fury that came from her direction, the answer would have to be no to both questions.

"What's all that noise?" asked Kermit.

"It's just New York," answered Rizzo with a shrug.

"Oh. Sure. Noisy town," commented Kermit. Then he said, "Jenny, I'm going to need your help with my costume. And Rizzo, you and the rats have a very important role to play tomorrow too." His friends drew closer, and Kermit gave them their instructions.

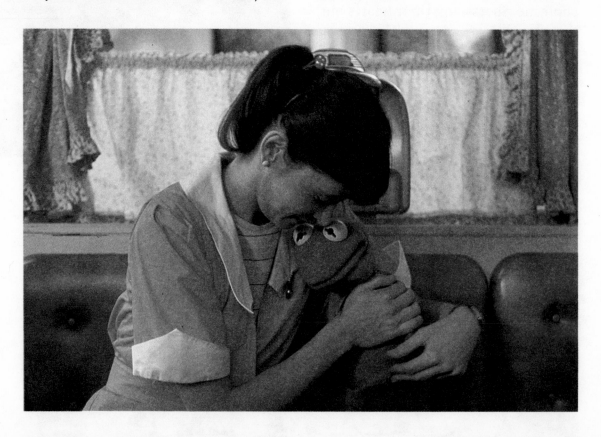

The next day an extremely elegant frog strolled into Sardi's at lunchtime. In his fancy fedora and fancy coat Kermit looked as important as anyone in the place, which was famous for being full of important people. He smiled graciously at the waiter who seated him.

As soon as the waiter turned away, Kermit quickly removed the photograph of the celebrity hanging on the wall behind him. Then he hung a picture of himself on the wall in its place.

Next he opened his coat, still smiling graciously, and Rizzo and the rats scurried out. They slid down the chair and ran under tables throughout the room. Then, at a signal from Kermit, they began to whisper. "Say, isn't that the rich producer Kermit the Frog?" one rat whispered, making sure that he was heard over the background noise of dishes and silverware and conversation. "It's him! The one who's investing in 'Manhattan Melodies,' " another hissed loudly.

"So *that's* the producer I've been hearing about recently," one diner remarked.

" 'Manhattan Melodies,' " a woman at the next table said to her husband. "Isn't that the new hit musical everyone's been talking about?" Heads turned to look at Kermit, who sat calmly under his picture, looking very much like a frog who was used to being looked at.

In minutes the whole room was buzzing with people talking about Kermit. The plan was working like a dream. Just then Vincent, the owner, came by, showing a famous celebrity to her table. "Vincent!" she cried, seeing Kermit's picture where hers used to be. "Did I do something wrong?"

It was at that very moment that Rizzo decided he was too hungry to last another second without a nibble. The other rats, who were also getting pretty hungry, followed him. Suddenly—in about the time it takes to scream "RATS!!!"—the whole place was turned upside down. Terrified diners jumped up on their chairs and went running for the exits, crashing into waiters and other diners. The rats were so frightened by all the noise

and excitement that *they* jumped up on the tables too. Soon there were rats and veal chops and trays whizzing all over the place. The only calm person in the room was an elderly gentleman who had fainted with fright and lay underneath his table, out cold.

In the middle of all the madness Vincent spotted the celebrity's picture on the seat next to Kermit. That was all the evidence he needed to link the frog with the riot in his restaurant.

The next thing the rats and the ex-famous frog producer knew, they were all out on their seats on the sidewalk. "That's it!" Kermit said defiantly. He picked himself up, slowly and painfully. "I've learned my lesson—I just can't be a phony anymore!" The rats shrugged, miserable and hungry, as Kermit announced, "I don't know what to do . . . but I do know what *not* to do!" Then he limped off, muttering to himself, and the rats followed dejectedly behind him.

The next day at lunchtime Piggy crouched behind a bush in Central Park. She wasn't thinking about lunch, and she certainly wasn't thinking about how pretty the park looked in the sunshine. She was too busy watching Kermit and Jenny, who were setting off on a jog in the park. And what she was thinking was *Oh, no, you don't! No one runs off with my frog!*

She took off after them, running through the bushes so they wouldn't see her. But even though she was very determined, she just wasn't cut out for leaping around at top speed in her high-heeled shoes. In minutes Piggy was collapsing against a lamppost, panting and gasping for air.

36

As she stood squinting at Kermit and Jenny in the distance, a hand reached around from behind her. Then it closed around her purse and yanked it away. The thief sprinted off.

"Right!! That does it!!" squealed the enraged Piggy. She turned to a skater sitting nearby. "May I borrow these?" she asked. Without waiting for an answer, she grabbed the skates and strapped them on. Then she took off after the thief, completely forgetting that she was out of breath.

She zoomed past walkers and strollers and skaters and cyclists. Meanwhile the thief had ducked behind a rock to empty Piggy's purse. He took out bonbons and binoculars

but couldn't find any money. Then he took out a hair dryer and makeup and four or five framed pictures of Kermit. Still no money. He was just taking out nine or ten fashion magazines when a terrifying scream split the air. Piggy came skating off the rocks above him at fantastic speed. She sailed through the air and landed on the thief with awesome force and a bloodcurdling shriek.

A policeman came running up to arrest the extremely surprised and extremely flattened criminal. Kermit and Jenny came jogging up behind him. "You're supposed to be out of

town!" Kermit cried, astonished. "What are you doing in New York?"

Piggy sniffed. "I really don't wish to discuss it in present company," she said, looking right at Jenny.

"I'll leave you two alone," Jenny said, and slipped quietly away.

"*Vous* is certainly looking different," said Piggy. "No shirt cut to the waist, no gold chains to impress a certain young lady."

Kermit was totally taken aback. "Were you *spying* on me, Piggy?" he asked, outraged. He started to explain that Jenny was just a friend who had been helping him.

Piggy interrupted. "Then what about the huggies?" she asked, her snout in the air.

"We were hugging because we're friends!" Kermit shot back. "Friends hug, but they do not spy!!"

"I spied because I care," Piggy yelled.

"Well, *I* care too!" Kermit yelled even louder. Then he held up his hand as Piggy was about to reply.

"Wait, wait a minute," he said very quietly to her. "Let's take a break." He called to the driver of a horse-drawn carriage nearby, and they climbed in.

Someone very wise once observed that there is nothing quite like a horse and carriage to turn an angry pig and frog into a pair of lovebirds. And that is exactly what Kermit and Piggy discovered as they rode around Central Park together.

"Oh, Kermy," Piggy cooed blissfully. "Imagine if we'd been teeny babies together, playing together the way teeny babies do."

Kermit thought for a moment. "Uh . . . actually, Piggy, I think a barnyard animal would have been a little out of place in our swamp."

Piggy smiled. "Now just close your eyes and imagine," she commanded gently. "There I am, a teensy weensy little piglet, falling snout over heels in love with the cutest, sweetest little tadpole in the whole wide world."

And the funny thing about it was that Kermit *could* see it.

"Look . . . there we are, happy little babies playing with our little baby friends. And planning a wonderful life together. Aren't I completely adorable?" Piggy asked.

Kermit, concentrating hard, nodded.

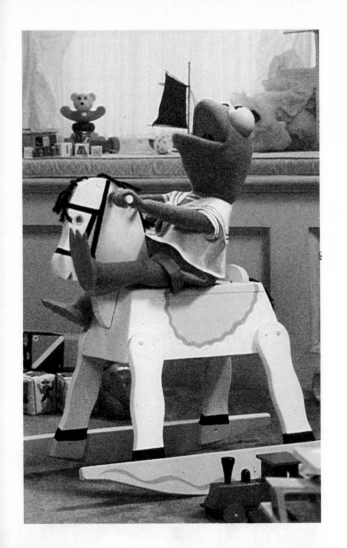

Meanwhile, many miles away, Rowlf had his paws full. He was managing a boarding kennel for other dogs. A rich gentleman was dropping his spoiled little pooch off and giving Rowlf the last of ninety-five instructions.

"Snooky gets his breakfast of quiche at eight A.M. exactly," the gentleman told him. "Good-bye, ittle lumpy dums," he sniffled to his pet. "Daddy's gonna miss ittle snooky wooky *so* much."

As soon as Rowlf convinced the man to leave, the other dogs stopped barking and started teasing the new arrival. "Does snooky wooky want his boney woney?" asked a big German shepherd sarcastically.

"Or would he like a teensy weensy bite of quiche?" snarled a mean-eyed Doberman.

"All right, you guys," called Rowlf. "Lay off him."

The dogs stopped teasing and started nagging Rowlf instead. "I need a walk," whined one.

"It's time for my brushing," called another.

"I wanna go home," howled a third. Then the whole kennel erupted in a deafening chorus of nagging, wailing, barking dogs.

Out in Ohio, Scooter also had his hands full. He had found a job managing a theater featuring *The Attack of the Killer Fish* in 3-D. The Swedish Chef was working at the popcorn and candy counter. He was busy throwing popcorn into the air, trying to give his customers a 3-D candy experience as they went in to see the film.

The movie started rolling and boomerang fish-thrower Lew Zealand waited for his moment. When the killer fish in the movie attacked the hero and heroine, he sprang into action. He reached into his bucket and started launching fish at the screen. Because he was a boomerang fish-thrower, the fish curved back and landed in the audience. "How realistic!" and "What a great 3-D effect!" they cried as they were bombarded with bass and slammed with salmon.

Back in New York, things at Pete's were quiet. Piggy was now working as a waitress there. She and Jenny were reading over Kermit's shoulder as he finished the postcards he'd gotten from Scooter and Rowlf.

"Just one more," said Jenny, handing Kermit an envelope. He opened it, and the three of them read it silently: "DEAR KERMIT THE FROG, I WOULD BE VERY INTERESTED IN TALKING WITH YOU ABOUT YOUR MUSICAL, 'MANHATTAN MELODIES.' PLEASE COME TO MY OFFICE AT YOUR EARLIEST CONVENIENCE. SINCERELY, BERNARD CRAWFORD."

"Bernard Crawford!" screamed Jenny, scaring Piggy and Kermit half to death. "I've heard of him! He's a big-time Broadway producer!"

Kermit was halfway out the door before she could say another word.

"Call us and tell us what happened!" Piggy shouted after him.

"Just act confident," added Jenny as Kermit whizzed down the street in a green blur.

In minutes Kermit stood outside Bernard Crawford's office. He was trying very hard to look confident when a young man walked up to him.

"Are you Kermit the Frog?" the young man asked.

"Yes . . . are you Bernard Crawford?"

"No," the young man replied a little nervously.

Kermit was trying to figure out what could possibly be going on when a distinguished-looking gentleman walked up.

"Dad," the young man said. "Re-

each other and jumped up and down, about as excited as a young producer and a frog can get. "I'll see you at Pete's!" Kermit shouted to Ronnie.

Then he dashed out onto the street, found a pay phone, and dialed Pete's. "Piggy, we did it! They're going to produce the show!" he yelled into the phone, loud enough for most of the people on the block to hear. "You're going to be a big star and Jenny can do the costumes . . . and we have to get the gang back right away!"

On the other end of the phone Jenny and Piggy cheered and hugged each other. "I'll be there in ten minutes!" Kermit called triumphantly.

member how you promised me my one chance to be a producer? Well, this is Kermit the Frog and I want to produce his musical."

Kermit could hardly believe that he was hearing these wonderful words. Before anyone could say anything else, he began telling Mr. Crawford about "Manhattan Melodies." "It's about how the two leads get married after they sing this song and my friends who are dogs and bears and chickens perform in it and . . ."

"That's ridiculous!" thundered the producer.

Kermit's legs turned to rubber. His jaw dropped open, his shoulders sagged, and his heart started to break.

"But," the producer added, "maybe 'ridiculous' is just what Broadway needs right now. Ronnie, you can do it!"

"Thanks, Dad!" yelled his son.

"Yeah! Thanks, Dad!" yelled Kermit. Kermit and Ronnie hugged

44

He went flying down the street, charged with happiness. He stepped off the curb, too busy singing and grinning and being deliriously excited to look up at the traffic light, which, unfortunately, was red. Kermit bounded straight out into the path of the speeding traffic.

And then it happened. With an awful squeal of brakes and a sickening thud, a taxi hit Kermit and sent him flying into the air. Onlookers gasped in horror as he crashed to the pavement. Kermit lay there, not speaking or even moving, as cars screeched to a halt and people rushed toward the accident.

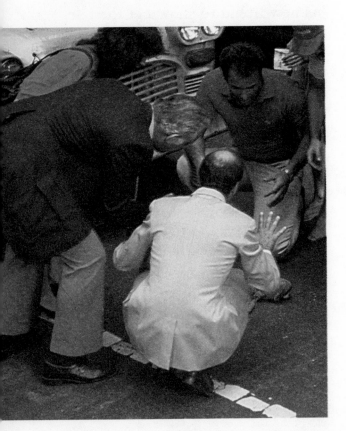

Hours later, Piggy was peering anxiously out of the door at Pete's. "He's *never* disappeared like this," she wailed. It was so late that the place was closed, and still there was no sign of Kermit.

As Piggy paced, sick with worry, Jenny tried to comfort her. "He's all right, Piggy. Why not think about how you'll be a big Broadway star in just a few months?" she suggested gently.

"Two weeks," a voice from the door corrected her. Everyone turned as a stranger stepped into Pete's. "I'm Ronnie Crawford," he said. "Your producer. My dad said I could have the theater, the sets, and everything—but only if we open in two weeks." It was only after the others

45

introduced themselves to him that Ronnie realized Kermit was missing. "The writer and star of the show is missing!" he gasped, suddenly a very worried young producer. "And we're opening in *two weeks*?!"

"No sweat," Jenny told Ronnie. "We'll find him." Then she and Pete sent telegrams to the others, telling them to hurry back to the city.

Way out in polka-crazy Monongahela, Pennsylvania, Dr. Teeth and the Electric Mayhem Band were crashing through the "We Never Ever Wanna Play Another Polka" polka when a telegram arrived. It took them about two seconds to get their instruments, Dr. Bunsen Honeydew, Beaker, and the gas-powered drumometer into their friend Bo's truck. Next stop, Broadway!

Up in a cave in Maine, Fozzie woke his new friend to show her the telegram that had just arrived. "Come with me," he suggested, forgetting for the moment that he was extremely shy.

"I will," the beautiful bear responded.

"What's going on? Is it spring yet?" the other bears asked, waking up.

"Follow me!" Fozzie shouted, and a sleepy bunch of bears followed him out of the cave.

On Lake Michigan, Gonzo rounded up his choral chicken chums. "Hey, girls," he told them, "we're going to New York!"

At the kennel, Rowlf barked an order to his canine companions: "Let's go, guys!"

In a certain extremely weird movie theater in Ohio, Scooter called "New York!" to the Swedish Chef and Lew Zealand. Before the popcorn and the fish in the air had landed, they were on their way.

While Scooter and Fozzie and Gonzo and all the others were speeding toward the city, a strange scene was unfolding in a Manhattan hospital room. Kermit sat in bed with a blank look on his face, listening to a doctor.

"You're absolutely fine physically, so we can't keep you here any longer," the doctor explained. "But because you've lost your memory, we just don't know who you are." She pulled out a pen light and began to wave it

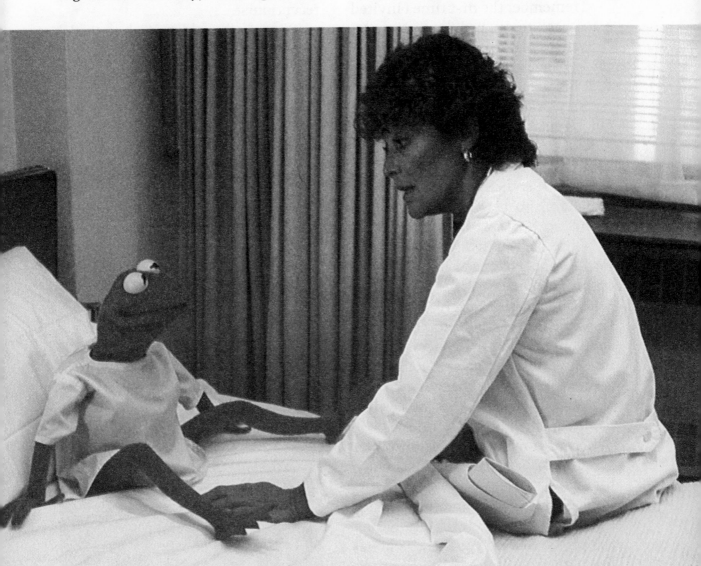

in front of Kermit's face. "Perhaps if I hypnotize you and take you back to your past, you just might remember who you are." Kermit went into a deep trance. "Good. Now, what's the first thing you recall?" the doctor asked.

"I remember my father croaking," Kermit told her.

"I'm so sorry. But what about when you were a teenager?"

"I remember the first time I invited a girl back to my pad."

"What did she call you?" the doctor asked, trying to get Kermit to reveal his name.

"She called me Snuggles. . . . Oh, Freida! Freida!" cried Kermit. "Freida . . . why don't you answer me?"

"Um . . . er, hello," the doctor said, pretending to be Kermit's lost girlfriend.

"Oh, Freida . . . you're so wonderful!" Kermit exclaimed, a dopey smile on his face.

"Yes, I am wonderful," the doctor responded, her mind racing. Maybe she could trick her mystery patient into revealing his identity. "So let's get married and I'll change my name to yours. By the way, what *is* your name?"

Kermit frowned. "Freida, how can you talk about getting married on our first date?"

The doctor sighed and snapped her fingers to bring Kermit out of his trance. "I'm afraid your case is hopeless," she told him. "All we can do

is wish you luck starting your new life."

Kermit felt a little lost that day as he left the hospital. He was wearing a new suit that the hospital had given him, and he was carrying the address of an advertising agency where the doctor had said he might find work. Within an hour he had found the office and was standing in front of the receptionist.

"Your name, please?" she asked.

It wasn't an unusual question, but to Kermit it was pretty hard to answer. "Um . . . Phil!" he blurted out, guessing wildly.

"And your last name, Phil?" she asked pleasantly.

Kermit thought as fast as he could. *Phil Harmonic? No, too weird. Phil Youmarryme? Too unusual . . .*

Before Kermit could admit that he had no idea what his name was, a smart-looking frog walked in. "I'm Bill, this is Will, and this is Jill," he said to Kermit, introducing two other businesslike frogs. "We'll show you around." The three took Kermit down the hall to the office where he would be working with them.

Across town at Pete's the whole gang was being reunited. A great deal of hugging and yelling went on, and after that quite a bit of introducing.

"The opening is just a week away, folks," Ronnie announced as he walked in. The introductions started all over again so that everyone could meet the producer. Finally Piggy called for quiet.

"Kermit is missing!" she told them, fighting back the tears.

"Oh, wow! Double bummer!" gasped Janice.

"I just can't believe it," said Fozzie.

"Missing! When? Where? How?" asked Gonzo.

Then they all started talking and asking questions at once. Though they were shocked and worried, Kermit's friends were sure about one thing—they were going to find him!

"What are we standing here for? Let's go!" shouted Scooter.

"Go! Go!" chanted Animal as the gang poured out of Pete's.

And so they started looking for Kermit. Scooter searched the streets on his bike and Gonzo looked in alleyways and in strange tunnels and passages. Animal roared Kermit's name at the zoo and Jenny checked the place in the park where she and Kermit had once jogged. Piggy peered hopefully into horse-drawn carriages while Dr. Teeth checked the library and Rowlf went up the Empire State Building.

Days went by, newspaper and radio advertisements announced the opening of "Manhattan Melodies," and the gang got nowhere. They checked the bus terminal where they had all started out. Nothing. They called out "Kermit!" in the streets so often that even the lampposts got sick of hearing it. Still nothing. They tried everything anybody could think of to try. And then there was absolutely nothing left to do and no time to do it in anyway.

"It's hopeless. Absolutely hopeless," said Piggy, who was heartbroken.

"And I always thought that opening night would be so exciting," added Fozzie. The others, sitting around a table at Pete's, didn't even respond. It was time to go to the theater and get ready for the first performance, but nobody moved a muscle. They were too miserable to budge. They were so utterly dejected that they didn't even look up when four frogs in suits came in and sat down at a booth.

Kermit sat at the table with Bill and Will and Jill. And soon he got the oddest feeling. He found himself tapping out a tune on the water glasses, a tune he didn't even know he knew. Strange.

The melody of one of the songs from "Manhattan Melodies" came wafting through the fog of gloom that surrounded the others. In a second a dozen heads were peering over the booth, staring at Bill and Jill. "Oh . . . just some frogs," someone said, and they sank back into their seats, disappointed once again.

But then a long beak went poking

around the side of the booth. An enormous Gonzoid shriek split the silence: "It's Kermit!!!" Suddenly Piggy and Jenny and Fozzie and Scooter and quite a few others were hugging Kermit and shouting questions at him and hugging him again.

"I believe there must be some mistake," Kermit said. "But please allow me to congratulate you on the friendly service," he added politely, seeing that he had disappointed them.

"Kermy . . . what's wrong?" Piggy wailed.

"Nothing that I can see," answered Kermit politely. "I think I'll have the tuna melt, an order of fries, and a cherry coke, please."

His friends began to get the idea that something about Kermit was very strange. "Kermit, don't you know us?" they asked him. "Don't you remember the show? It's opening night tonight."

Kermit shrugged. "A show sounds amusing enough, but I do have some marketing data to review this evening," he replied.

Piggy whispered an urgent command to the others. Then she yelled, "Grab him!" and they pounced on Kermit and carried him out of Pete's.

Above the theater the marqee glowed with a big, bright sign: "MAN-HATTAN MELODIES" BY KERMIT THE FROG. The name of their show was up in lights, just as they had dreamed. But backstage, things weren't going as well. In fact, they weren't going anywhere. The situation was desperate. First Fozzie had tried to get Kermit to remember his friends by telling him his favorite Fozzie jokes, but Kermit had just smiled politely.

"Very amusing, but I really must be off," he said.

Next Gonzo pulled out four balloons, a ukulele, a set of bagpipes, and a tin ear flute. And then he performed Kermit's favorite Gonzo trick. He strummed "Honolulu Harry" on the ukulele while blowing up the balloons with the bagpipes and doing imitation bird calls with the ear flute.

"Quite an accurate rendition of a cardinal's call," said Kermit as Gonzo bounced up and down on the wheezing bagpipes and tweeted the ear flute. "An *unusual* imitation, but quite accurate, nevertheless," he repeated. Gonzo gave up.

Even Statler and Waldorf were brought in. They tried to prod Kermit's memory with their silly insults. "Are those your eyes, or did you sit too close to a Ping-Pong game?" they asked.

"As I mentioned earlier," Kermit said evenly, "I do have a rather important board meeting in the morning."

Before long it was time for Dr. Teeth and the Electric Mayhem Band to start the overture. It was time to admit defeat. After all they had been through together. After all the no's from all

the producers, and after all the happiness of thinking they had finally made it.

But Piggy would not give up. "Look at me," she commanded, staring into Kermit's eyes. "You are Kermit the Frog. These are your friends. You wrote this show for them." Kermit listened politely. "And you love me. You want to marry me."

Suddenly Kermit laughed. "What!?" he cried. "In love with a pig?" He seemed genuinely amused at the idea. "You've got to be kidding! Think I've gone hog-wild? I'd have to be a bit rasher to do that! Get it?" He giggled and slapped his knee. "Maybe you could bring home the bacon!"

A pair of pig eyes flashed with fury. There was a sudden blur of pink and a killer karate chop sent Kermit hurtling across the room and crashing against the far wall.

He lay still, a tangle of twisted arms and bent flippers. Then slowly, very

slowly, he opened his eyes, blinked, and shut them again.

And snapped upright. "Piggy! Fozzie! Jenny! Where am I?" His friends exploded with excitement, their whoops of joy mingling with the sounds of the overture being played in the theater. "He's back!" and "You know you're Kermit!" they yelled at the confused frog.

"What's going on?" Kermit demanded.

"*You* are!" Ronnie answered, leading him out of the dressing room. "This is Broadway. We've made it. Remember the opening song?"

"Sure, but the show is still missing something," said Kermit slowly. "It's not quite ready."

He was interrupted by his friends from the advertising agency. "Can we watch?" they asked Kermit.

"No!" Kermit cried. "Because you're going to be in the show . . . all of you!" He waved his arms to include Fozzie's bear friends and Rowlf's dogs and Camilla's chicken choir companions and all the others who had come to New York. "*All* of you! More chickens and frogs and dogs and *everything* is just what the show has been missing. Come on!"

Then he grabbed Piggy's hand. And as the band played the first song, Kermit danced out onto the stage with Scooter and Fozzie and Gonzo and Rowlf and Camilla.

"Look at us. Here we are, right where we belong," they sang as the audience applauded and the curtain rose. The lights came up on the set, which was a beautiful model of the streets of New York, with rats and bears and dogs playing the parts of police officers and tourists and door-men and just plain New Yorkers. Jenny's costumes looked sensational and the band had never sounded bet-ter—"Manhattan Melodies" felt like a Broadway smash.

"Extra! Extra!" a dog shouted on-stage. "Somebody's getting married!" He started handing out newspapers, and everybody took up the cry.

As they sang, Fozzie and Gonzo and Scooter took Kermit to a tailor's shop on one side of the stage. There the tailor fitted him out as the groom. And at the same time Piggy was being outfitted with a beautiful bridal gown. Piggy and Kermit were going to get married in the musical.

Practically everybody had come to join in the big scene. All the Muppet friends and family from near and far waited in the chapel. And then Kermit walked in, looking as hand-some as any frog ever looked on his wedding day.

But Piggy looked more than handsome. She radiated, she glowed, she shone with happiness. Everyone in the audience sighed and smiled at how beautiful a bride she made.

As everyone in the chapel sang about the bride and the groom, Piggy arrived at the altar and smiled at Kermit. "I only know he'll make me happy," she sang softly, "and that's all I ever need to know."

As Kermit and Piggy knelt at the

altar, the minister stepped forward to begin the ceremony. "Piggy," Kermit whispered, "I thought Gonzo was going to play the minister."

Before Piggy could answer, the minister began to speak. "Do you, Piggy, take this frog to be your lawful wedded husband?"

"I do!" she sang out joyfully.

He turned to Kermit. "Do you, Froggie, take this pig to be your lawful wedded wife?"

"Well, I...well...er..." Kermit answered nervously. The entire audience hushed as Kermit gulped. "I do," he sang.

Then the minister intoned, "Be-cause you share a love so big, I now pronounce you—frog and pig."

Piggy turned to Kermit and they kissed. As their lips touched, bells rang out and hundreds of doves flew upward in the chapel. And everybody cheered, cried, laughed, and jumped for joy. The rats danced deliriously, Jenny hugged Ronnie, and Pete hugged himself.

In the middle of the excitement Kermit leaned over to Gonzo, who was playing his best man. "Hey, Gonzo!" he whispered. "Why didn't you play the minister? And who was that actor who took your place?"

"That was no actor," Gonzo corrected him. "That was a real minister."

"Piggy!" Kermit yelled.

"Oh, Kermy, I'm so happy!" Piggy cried, and she did look happy. Very happy. Very, *very* happy.

Kermit gulped. But then he took her hand and smiled. "What better way could anything end, hand in hand with a friend?" he sang. And with all their friends around them onstage, he drew Piggy close and kissed his new bride.